A NOTE TO PARENTS

When your children are ready to "step into reading," giving them the right books—and lots of them—is as crucial as giving them the right food to eat. **Step into Reading Books** present exciting stories and information reinforced with lively, colorful illustrations that make learning to read fun, satisfying, and worthwhile. They are priced so that acquiring an entire library of them is affordable. And they are beginning readers with an important difference—they're written on four levels.

Step 1 Books, with their very large type and extremely simple vocabulary, have been created for the very youngest readers. **Step 2 Books** are both longer and slightly more difficult. **Step 3 Books,** written to mid-second-grade reading levels, are for the child who has acquired even greater reading skills. **Step 4 Books** offer exciting nonfiction for the increasingly proficient reader.

Children develop at different ages. **Step into Reading Books,** with their four levels of reading, are designed to help children become good—and interested—readers *faster*. The grade levels assigned to the four steps—preschool through grade 1 for Step 1, grades 1 through 3 for Step 2, grades 2 and 3 for Step 3, and grades 2 through 4 for Step 4—are intended only as guides. Some children move through all four steps very rapidly; others climb the steps over a period of several years. These books will help your child "step into reading" in style!

To Bartley Jacob, who is just getting his teeth
–J. C.

To Ira & James August
–M. H.

Library of Congress Cataloging-in-Publication Data:
Cole, Joanna. The missing tooth / by Joanna Cole ; illustrated by Marylin Hafner.
p.   cm.–(Step into reading. A Step 2 book) SUMMARY: Best friends Arlo and Robby
are almost identical in what they wear, what they like, and even where they
have teeth missing, but when Robby insists on betting on who is going to lose
the next tooth, their friendship is endangered.   ISBN: 0-394-89279-8 (pbk.);
0-394-99279-2 (lib. bdg.)   [1. Friendship–Fiction.   2. Teeth–Fiction.] I. Hafner,
Marylin, ill. II. Title. III. Series: Step into reading. Step 2 book.   PZ7.C67346As
1988 [E]–dc19   88-1903

Manufactured in the United States of America   36 35 34 33

Step into Reading

The Missing Tooth

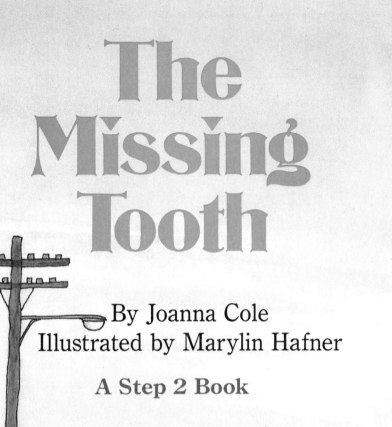

By Joanna Cole
Illustrated by Marylin Hafner

A Step 2 Book

Random House 🏠 New York

4

Arlo and Robby were best friends.

They both rode green bikes

with horns that went WONKA-WONKA.

They both had ant farms

and horned toads.

 They both liked

 to trade baseball cards.

And they both <u>loved</u>
peanut butter ice cream.

Arlo said,

"I think we are best friends
because we are so much alike.
We even have a tooth missing
in the same place."

One day at school
their teacher said,
"Arlo and Robby,
look at you today!"

Arlo and Robby laughed.

They both had on

blue Robot Man shirts,

red pants,

and black sneakers.

Arlo put his arm around Robby.

He said,

"We match all over.

Even our teeth match."

Then Arlo and Robby

both smiled a big smile

so everyone could see.

Later Robby and Arlo

were playing checkers.

Robby said,

"Guess what?

My other front tooth

is loose."

He wiggled his tooth.

Arlo wanted to be

the same as Robby.

He tried to wiggle his tooth.

"I think mine is loose too,"

he said.

But it really wasn't.

"Let's make a bet,"
said Robby.
"If my tooth comes out first,
you have to give me ten cents.
If your tooth comes out first,
I have to give you ten cents.
Is it a deal?"
Arlo did not want
to make the deal.
But he said yes anyway.
They shook on it.

A few days later,

Robby went to Arlo's house.

They were going to trade baseball cards.

Robby had a Pete Rose card.

"I wish I had a Pete Rose card,"
said Arlo.

"Will you trade it?"

Robby shook his head.

"No, Arlo," he said.

"It is my best card.

I cannot trade it."

Arlo got up.

"I am hungry," he said.

"Let's not trade cards

anymore."

Arlo got two apples.

He gave one to Robby.

They sat outside together.

Robby bit into his apple.

He put his hand over his mouth.

"Look, Arlo!

My other tooth came out!"

Robby held out his hand.

The tooth was in it.

"Gee," said Arlo.

"That's neat.

But now we are not the same."

Robby did not seem to hear.

He saw Mr. Walker go by.

"Mr. Walker!" shouted Robby.

"I just lost a tooth!"

"Well, well,"

said Mr. Walker.

"The tooth fairy will be

coming to your house tonight!"

"With my tooth fairy money

I can buy more baseball cards,"

said Robby.

Then Robby looked at Arlo.

"Hey. I almost forgot.

We had a bet.

My tooth came out first.

You have to give me ten cents."

Arlo gave Robby the money.

But he was mad.

Robby was going to get money

from the tooth fairy.

Robby was going to get

<u>more</u> baseball cards.

And Robby already

<u>had</u> a Pete Rose card.

It was not fair.

Robby had everything!

Arlo went into the backyard.

Robby followed him.

Arlo began to swing on his tire.

"Can I swing too?" asked Robby.

"No," said Arlo.

"Let's play ball,"
said Robby.
"I don't want to,"
said Arlo.
"If you will not play,"
said Robby,
"I am going home."

"Hurry up," said Arlo.

"Don't keep the tooth fairy waiting!"

"You are mean,"

said Robby.

"I don't want to play

with you anymore!"

And Robby went home.

Arlo went inside.

He made a tower of blocks.

Then he pushed it down.

He felt as lonely

as his one space in front.

The next day,
Arlo did not say hello
to Robby.

At show and tell,

Robby showed

his tooth money.

He also showed

his box of baseball cards.

"I am going to buy

more baseball cards today,"

said Robby.

After show and tell,

Robby put away his baseball cards.

One fell out.

Robby did not see it.

But Arlo did.

Arlo picked it up.

It was the Pete Rose card!

Arlo wanted to keep the card.

He almost put it

in his pocket.

Then he looked at Robby.

It was Robby's card.

He would be sad

without it.

It was wrong

for Arlo to take it.

Robby was feeding the fish.

Arlo went over to him.

"Here, Robby," said Arlo.

"You dropped this."

"Gee, thanks, Arlo,"

said Robby.

Robby went and put the card

in his box.

"I am sorry we had a fight,"

Robby said.

Arlo nodded.

"Me too," he said.

Robby took something

out of his pocket.

It was ten cents.

"Take this back,"

said Robby.

"It was stupid

to make a bet."

Arlo thought for a moment.

Then he said,

"No. You keep it.

A bet is a bet.

Come on. Let's go play."

Arlo and Robby ran out
to the junglegym.

They climbed up to the top.

Arlo hung upside down.

His mouth bumped

on the bar.

Arlo sat up.

His hand was over his mouth.

"Robby, look at this!"

cried Arlo.

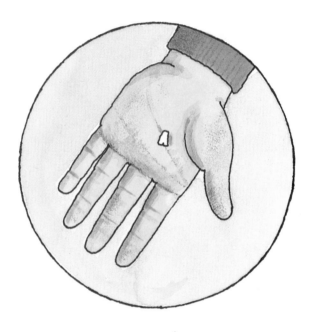

Arlo held out his hand.

There was a tooth in it.

"Now we have matching teeth again," said Robby.

"No, we don't," said Arlo.

Arlo opened his mouth.

The hole was in

a different place.

Arlo and Robby
both smiled a big smile.
They did not
have matching teeth.
But they were best friends anyway.